ICY'S ADVENTURE FREEZING THE HEAT

Written by Ben Levey

Illustrated by Salsabila Tata

Icy's Home in the Freezer In a freezer lived Icy, a tiny ice cube, Surrounded by friends, all in a happy group. They loved their COLD HOME and never wished to stray, But one hot day, something made them MELT away.

A Scary Escape Icy and friends felt scared and alone, But a kind hand saved them and took them home. They landed in a glass of water so COOL, And it was then that they met a water droplet jeweL.

Learning about GLOBAL WARMING The droplet explained about global warming, A phenomenon that was not very charming. It made the Earth HOTTER and MELTED the ice, Affecting habitats of creatures that weren't nice.

The Start of an Adventure Icy was curious and wanted to know more, So he set out on an adventure, not like before. He met animals who were affected by the heat, Their homes were vanishing, and they struggled to eat.

Taking Action Icy knew he had to take
some action, To save his home and prevent
more DESTRUCTION. He asked his friends
in the freezer to be aware, Turn off the
lights and show they care.

A Cool Movement Icy's message spread
far and wide, More ice cubes joined, with a
sense of pride. They all CONSERVED energy
and RECYCLED more, Helping the Earth and
its creatures, for sure.

A Changing Planet Thanks to Icy and his friends' hard work, The Earth got COOLER, and the ice caps didn't lurk. The animals had their homes back, and they THRIVED, All thanks to Icy, who showed he had arrived.

A Celebratory Return Icy returned to the glass of water with glee, His aDVeNTURe made him WiSeR, and he could see. He met his old and new friends, and they cheered, For Icy, who proved that small actions are revered.

A New Journey Begins Icy's adventure was over, but his heart was not done, He had more to explore, and more to have fun. He set out on a NEW JOURNEY, to help even more, And discover what the world had in store.

A Never-Ending Quest Icy knew his journey would never end, For the Earth needed help, and he had to extend. His efforts inspired others, and together they all, Worked towards a BETTER WORLD, one that was not small.

Printed in Great Britain
by Amazon

22272817R00016